A TALE OF THE ALASKAN GOLD RUSH

by J. Gunderson
illustrated by Shannon Townsend

Librarian Reviewer
Laurie K. Holland
Media Specialist (National Board Certified), Edina, MN
MA in Elementary Education, Minnesota State University, Mankato

Reading Consultant
Elizabeth Stedem
Educator/Consultant, Colorado Springs, CO
MA in Elementary Education, University of Denver, CO

 STONE ARCH BOOKS
Minneapolis   San Diego

Graphic Flashbacks are published by Stone Arch Books,
151 Good Counsel Drive, P.O. Box 669,
Mankato, Minnesota 56002.
www.stonearchbooks.com

Library of Congress Cataloging-in-Publication Data
Gunderson, Jessica.
    Fire and Snow: A Tale of the Alaskan Gold Rush / by J. Gunderson; illustrated by
Shannon Townsend.
    p. cm. — (Graphic Flash)
    ISBN-13: 978-1-59889-310-6 (library binding)
    ISBN-10: 1-59889-310-6 (library binding)
    ISBN-13: 978-1-59889-405-9 (paperback)
    ISBN-10: 1-59889-405-6 (paperback)
    1. Graphic novels. 2. Gold mines and mining—Alaska—Comic books, strips, etc.
I. Townsend, Shannon. II. Title.
PN6727.G777F57 2007
741.5'973—dc22   2006028031

Summary: The rivers of Alaska are flowing with gold! At least that's the story Ethan
Michelson hears from excited prospectors. He and his family leave their comfortable
home in Seattle to seek their fortune in the snowy North. Ethan must brave an avalanche,
cross an icy river, and battle a deadly fire before he can decide if the hunt for treasure is
worth the risk.

Art Director: Heather Kindseth
Graphic Designer: Brann Garvey

1 2 3 4 5 6 11 10 09 08 07 06

Printed in the United States of America.

TABLE OF CONTENTS

INTRODUCING . . .

Eliza Michelson

Robert Michelson

Cassie Michelson

Sugar Gold Charlie

Ethan Michelson

5

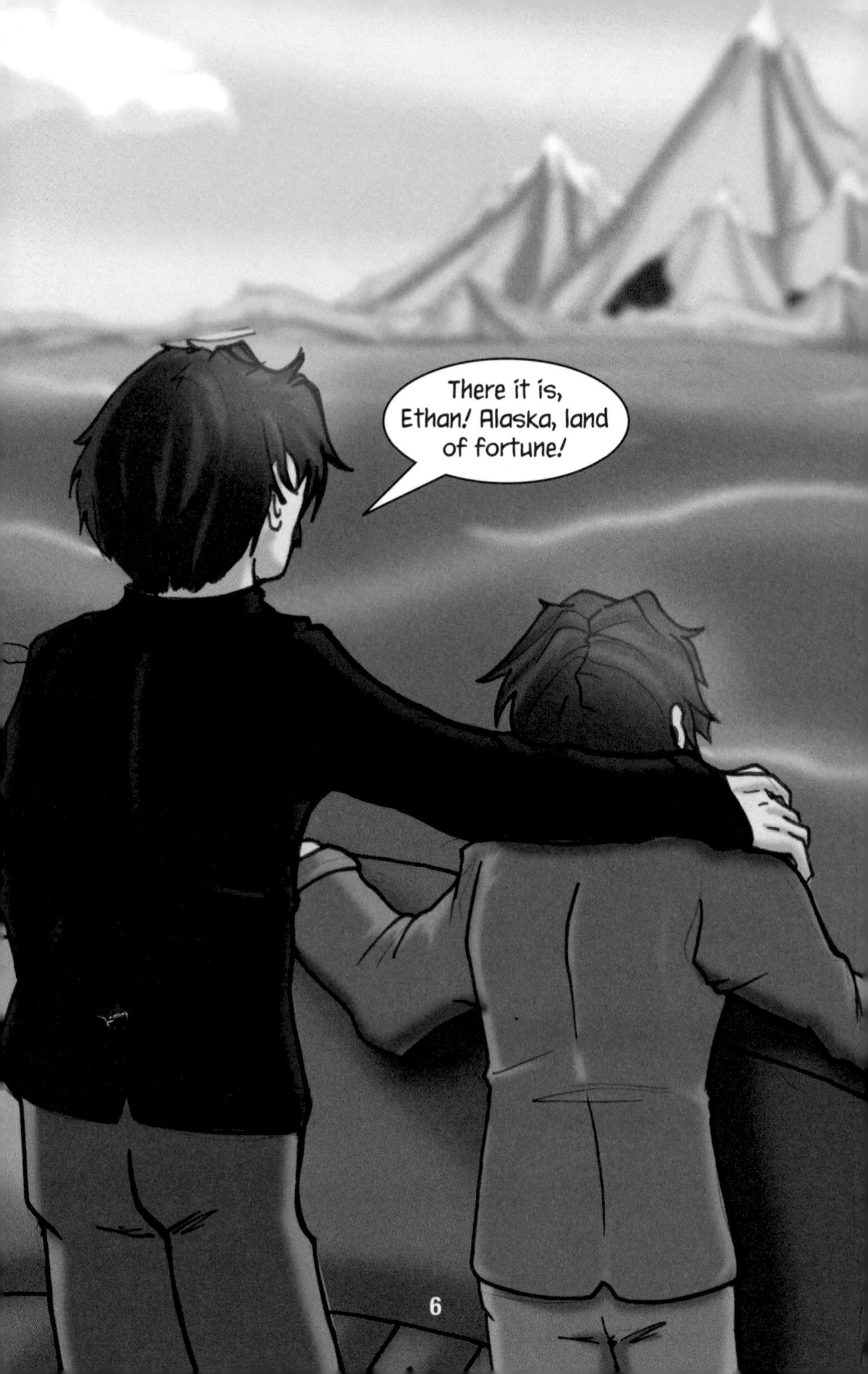
There it is, Ethan! Alaska, land of fortune!

Chapter 1

LAND OF FORTUNE

It was dawn on a cold day in October, 1897, when I had my first glimpse of Alaska. Icy waves crashed against our steamship, *The Stampede*, as we neared the coast. The distant, snowy mountains loomed ever closer and looked bigger with each passing moment.

I couldn't contain the excitement inside me. "I'm going to tell Mom and Cassie," I told Dad. "We're about to reach shore!"

They were seasick again and were asleep on the lower deck. I hoped they'd be as excited as I was about seeing Alaska, but I had my doubts.

First, let me explain how our journey north began. Just a few months ago, we'd been living in Seattle, Washington. There was a depression in the U.S., and nobody had money to spend at my father's dry goods store. So we were broke.

One day in July, Dad and I were walking home along the waterfront when we saw a steamship pulling up to the docks.

The Klondike region was far north, in Alaska and Canada. Luckily, the U.S. owned Alaska, so we could hunt for gold there if we wanted. We had heard stories that gold ran like water in Alaska.

Sugar Gold Charlie also told us how bitterly cold and dangerous Alaska was. He warned us to be prepared.

"Just think, son," Dad said as we headed toward home. His face was bright with excitement. "We'll make a fortune! We'll be rich! We'll be millionaires!"

Mom wasn't excited at all when she heard Dad's plan.

Finally, late into the night, and after many tears, Mom agreed to go to Alaska, but only if we'd return after one year.

I whooped with joy. We'd be leaving boring old Seattle for a new adventure!

The only downfall was that Cassie was also going. She was more than just a little sister. She was also a pain in the neck.

We weren't the only ones who heard about gold in Alaska. Hundreds of other folks were scrambling to buy tickets for the steamship *The Stampede.* Everyone seemed to have caught the Klondike gold fever.

After he sold the store, Dad and I searched Seattle for supplies we'd need, like food, and a tent, and a lantern.

Several days later, we boarded *The Stampede* and set out to sea.

And now, after so many weeks, we were finally reaching Alaska, land of gold and riches galore!

I found Mom and Cassie deep inside the dark, clammy belly of the ship. Other seasick passengers were down there too. I told them all the exciting news. They were delighted to hear we were about to dock.

"In Alaska I won't be seasick anymore," Cassie groaned happily.

"I can't wait," said Mom. But I could tell she didn't mean it.

"But aren't you excited about finding gold?" I asked.

"This is just another of your father's schemes to get rich," Mom said. "How can I be happy about that?"

Just then, I heard a thump. The ship had hit land!

Mom, Cassie, and I raced to the upper deck for our first look at Dyea, Alaska.

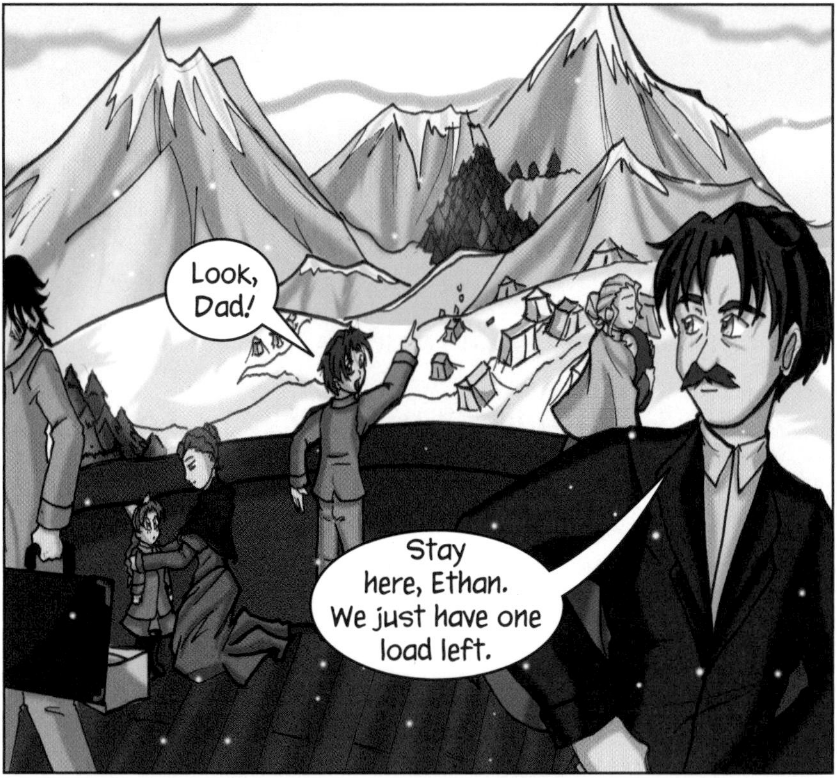
Look, Dad!
Stay here, Ethan. We just have one load left.

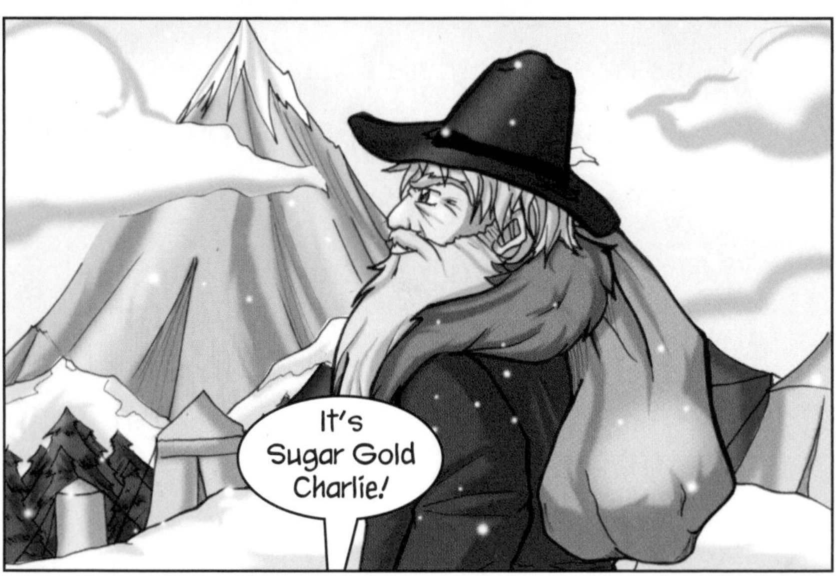
It's Sugar Gold Charlie!

I couldn't believe it! A familiar face in the middle of all these strangers!

"Sugar Gold Charlie!" I called.

He grinned and walked over.

"What are you doing here?" I asked.

"Same thing you are," he said. "Looking for gold."

"But don't you have enough?"

Charlie sighed. "That's the thing about gold, kid. Once you have a little, you always want more."

Charlie stared at our pile of belongings. "Is all this stuff yours?" he asked. "If it is, you better get rid of it."

"Why?" I asked.

Charlie pointed straight ahead. "To get to the gold," he said, "first you have to climb that!"

Chapter 2
A DANGEROUS FIRST STEP

When she saw the mountain we had to climb in the distance, Mom begged us to catch the next ship back to Seattle.

"Give it a chance, Eliza," Dad said. "Just over that mountain, riches await!"

We hadn't even gone ten feet before Cassie started complaining

"I'm tired and cold," she cried. "And hungry."

Before we reached the mountain, we had another obstacle. The trail led us to an icy river. As we watched the gold hunters ahead of us, we saw there was only one way across, and that was by foot.

The river was cold as ice. The waves knocked against my knees. As long as I stepped carefully and slowly, I thought I'd be okay.

But I was wrong. Halfway across the river, a strong current pulled my feet out from under me.

My legs had turned to ice. I couldn't kick or swim. I was at the mercy of the current. I was doomed.

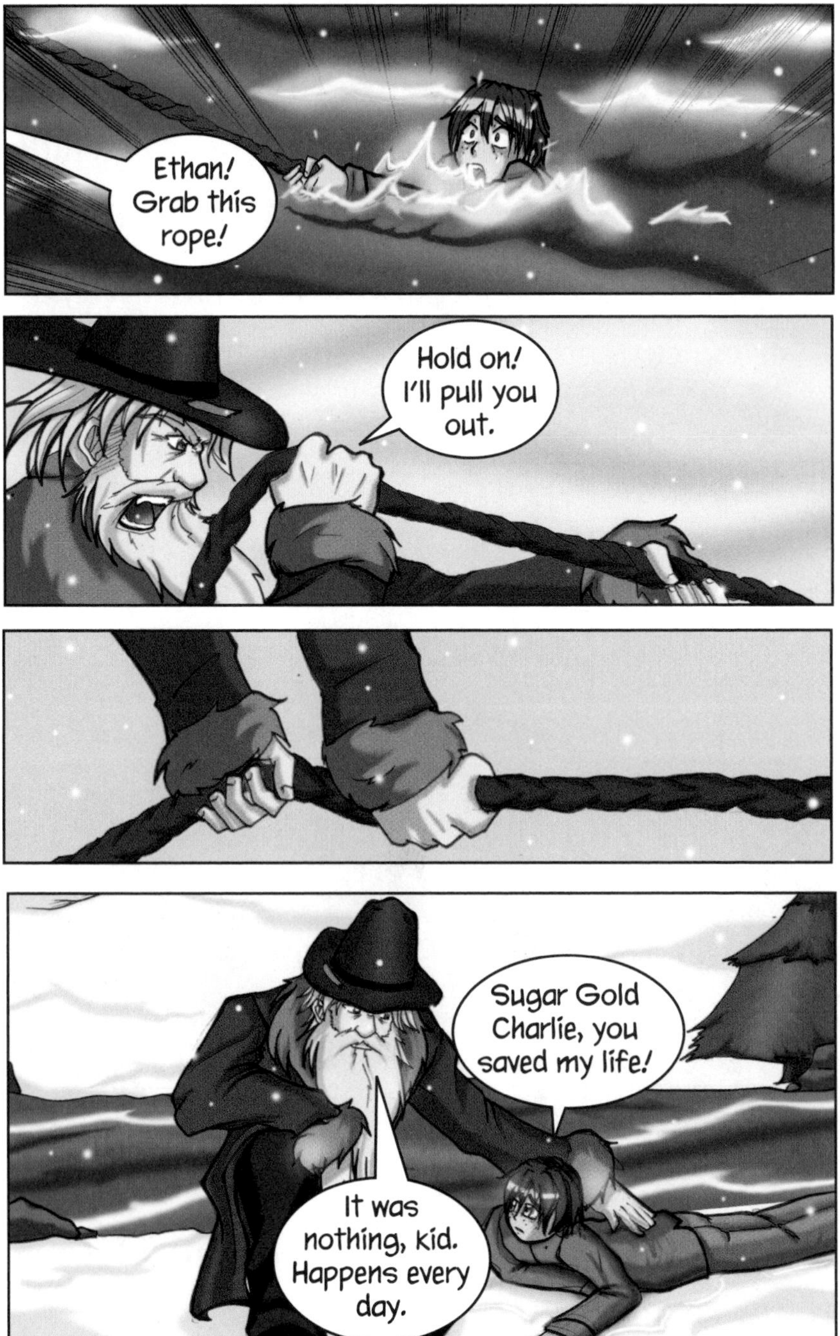
Ethan! Grab this rope!
Hold on! I'll pull you out.
Sugar Gold Charlie, you saved my life!
It was nothing, kid. Happens every day.

I heard my family running toward me. Mom cried when she saw that I was still alive. She wasn't even mad like I thought she might be.

Dad shook Sugar Gold Charlie's hand and thanked him for rescuing me.

"I'd better be on my way," Charlie said. "See you on the other side of the mountain."

Then he vanished into the falling snow.

It was nightfall by the time we reached Sheep Camp. We ate a hot meal at the inn, then hunkered down in our tent for some rest. I tumbled into a deep sleep, wondering what adventures the next day would bring.

Chapter 3

AVALANCHE

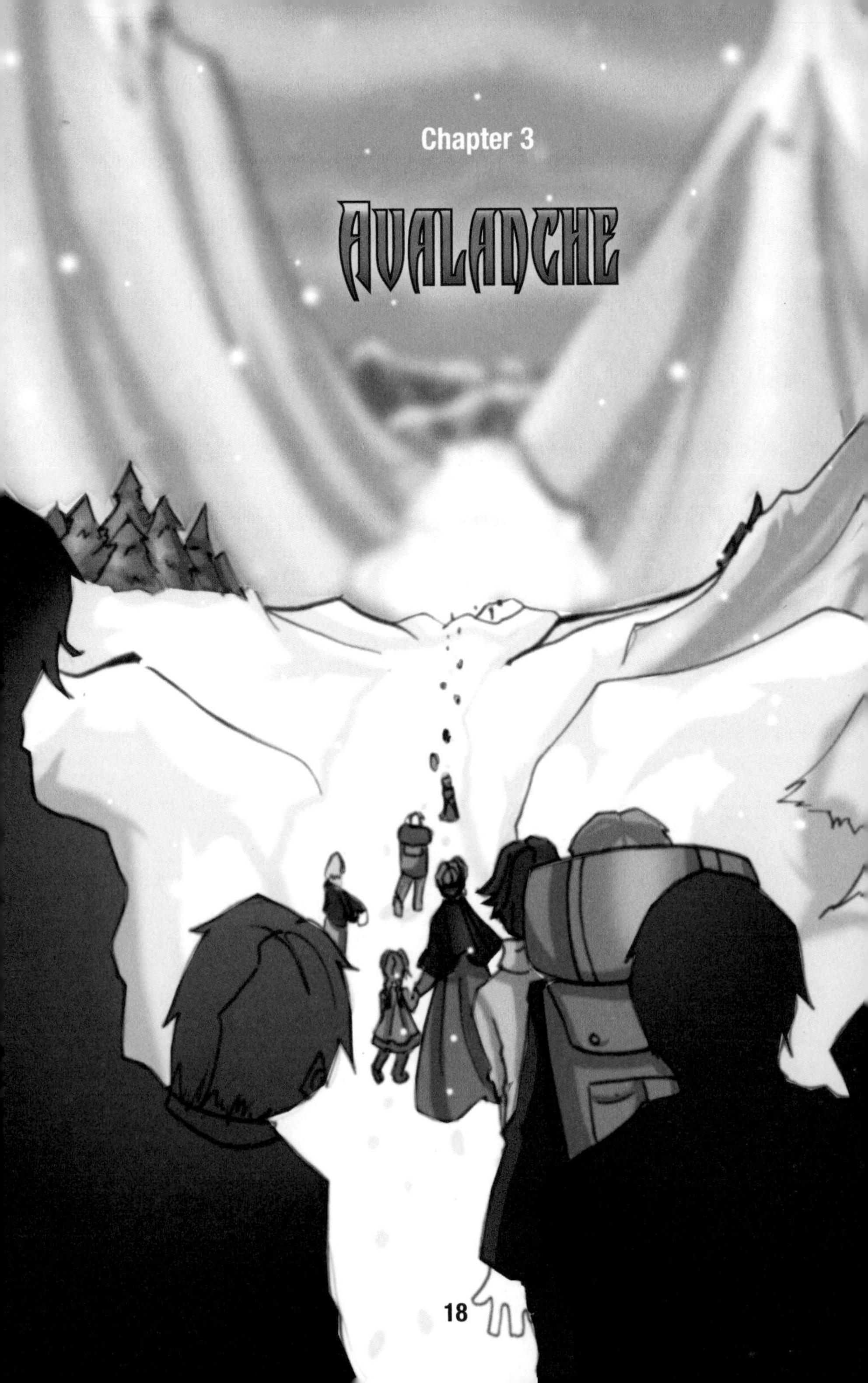

I awoke to a bright sun and the most magnificent sight I'd ever seen: Chilkoot Pass.

"Come on, kids," Dad called. "Let's gather our gear and start the climb."

"Do we really have to climb that big mountain?" Cassie whispered to me. "It looks so steep and scary."

"Don't worry," I said, swinging my pack over my shoulder. "We'll be at the top in no time."

Over the next half hour or so, we climbed up the pass. I hurried as fast as I could. I wasn't supposed to leave Cassie, but I knew she'd be right behind me. I saw a group of men in uniform along the way. They were the North West Police.

As I neared the top of the pass, I heard a dreadful noise. It sounded like thunder roaring and dogs growling and trains rumbling, all at once.

I finally reached the spot where I'd last seen her. But she was nowhere to be seen.

Then, on a pile of snow, I saw something that made my skin crawl.

I kept on digging, tears freezing on my cheeks. She had to be alive. She had to be!

Then, I struck something soft. "I think I feel her arm!" I screamed.

"Grab it and pull," one of the men commanded.

But I didn't want to. What if she was dead under all that snow?

Cassie was alive, but just barely. She had almost died because of me.

Why hadn't I stayed by her? If I had, maybe I could've pulled her to safety before the avalanche struck.

I had been too excited to get to the top first, to look around. The excitement of the people around me had somehow gotten inside me, too, like a worm digging into an apple. Maybe I had caught the gold fever that Sugar Gold Charlie talked about.

At the top, we found our parents. Boy, were they a sight for sore eyes!

Mom hugged us so tightly, our frozen bones nearly crunched together. When she let go, she gave my dad an angry glare.

"Is gold worth the safety of our children?" she asked.

Dad looked sad. He didn't answer.

I was beginning to agree with Mom. Our grand adventure was turning into a nightmare. Would we all make it to gold country alive?

Chapter 4

A GOLD-DIGGER'S PARADISE

The land of gold was drawing near, but after we crossed Chilkoot Pass, we had to spend the winter camped at Lake Lindeman. We had to wait for the Yukon River to thaw. When the ice broke, our excitement grew. Gold fever had struck again.

The next stage in our journey was Dawson City. We got there by boat.

"I hope we're not too late," Dad said as we reached the port. "What if all the claims have been taken?"

We were in luck. As we carried our belongings through the muddy streets, hunting for a place to stay, I saw a familiar face. It was Sugar Gold Charlie, my hero.

Dad promised that we'd go out to our claim first thing in the morning. We pitched our tent on the edge of town. Soon we'd start building a cabin.

That night I couldn't sleep. Dawson City is so far north that during the summer, the sun never sets. All night, the midnight sun burned through the tent.

Dawson City was a gold-digger's paradise. The next morning, we bought everything we needed to dig for gold: a pick and a shovel, a sluice box, and a poke, which was a pouch to keep our gold in.

Sugar Gold Charlie came along when we headed to our claim.

Finally, after a couple hours of walking, Dad and Charlie stopped beside a small stream. Dad looked at his map. "This is it!" he cried.

"Here?" I asked. "Where's the gold?"

Sugar Gold Charlie just smiled as Dad said, "Start digging, son."

I dug into the soft dirt next to the creek. Charlie told me to fill my pan with dirt. Then he told me to run cold water from the stream into the pan to separate the dirt from the gold.

Even though it was only dust, I emptied the pan into my poke. Gold was gold. I couldn't wait to show Mom and Cassie.

"The real gold is at least ten feet below the ground," said Dad.

"We'll be rich!" I said.

"Not so fast, son," said Dad. "We won't know until next spring. That's when we run the creek water through our sluice box."

Next spring? But it was only July. Spring seemed like a lifetime away.

That night at dinner, Cassie and I faced another disappointment.

"In one month you'll be starting school," Dad told us.

School? Cassie and I looked at each other in surprise. We hadn't known there would be school in Dawson City.

"But I want to help dig for gold," I said.

"In spring, you can help. But for now, you'll be in school all day," Dad said.

I groaned. I'd rather face another avalanche than go back to school.

We built a cabin on the edge of Dawson City. All winter long, Cassie and I attended school while Mom and Dad dug up our gold field.

I woke one spring morning, my heart thumping. Today was the day! It was spring clean-up, the day we'd finally see how much gold we'd dug.

The sluice box was ready. All we needed to do was run water down the box. The dirt would rinse away, and our gold would be stuck in the riffles, which were the ridges along the bottom of the box.

After all the dirt was gone, I looked into the sluice box. The bottom was filled with so much glittering gold that my eyes hurt to look at it.

All of our hardships were worth it. We'd discovered our fortune at last.

Chapter 5
A Thief in the Night

After we had finished cleaning the gold, we hauled it to our cabin. Cassie and I each got to keep two pokes filled with gold. I put mine under my bed.

Dad promised we could spend our gold on anything we wanted. I already knew what I was going to buy. A dog. A big Alaskan husky.

It seemed as if everyone in Dawson uncovered gold that spring. One night, the whole town had a celebration.

I'd never seen Dad so happy. His dream had come true.

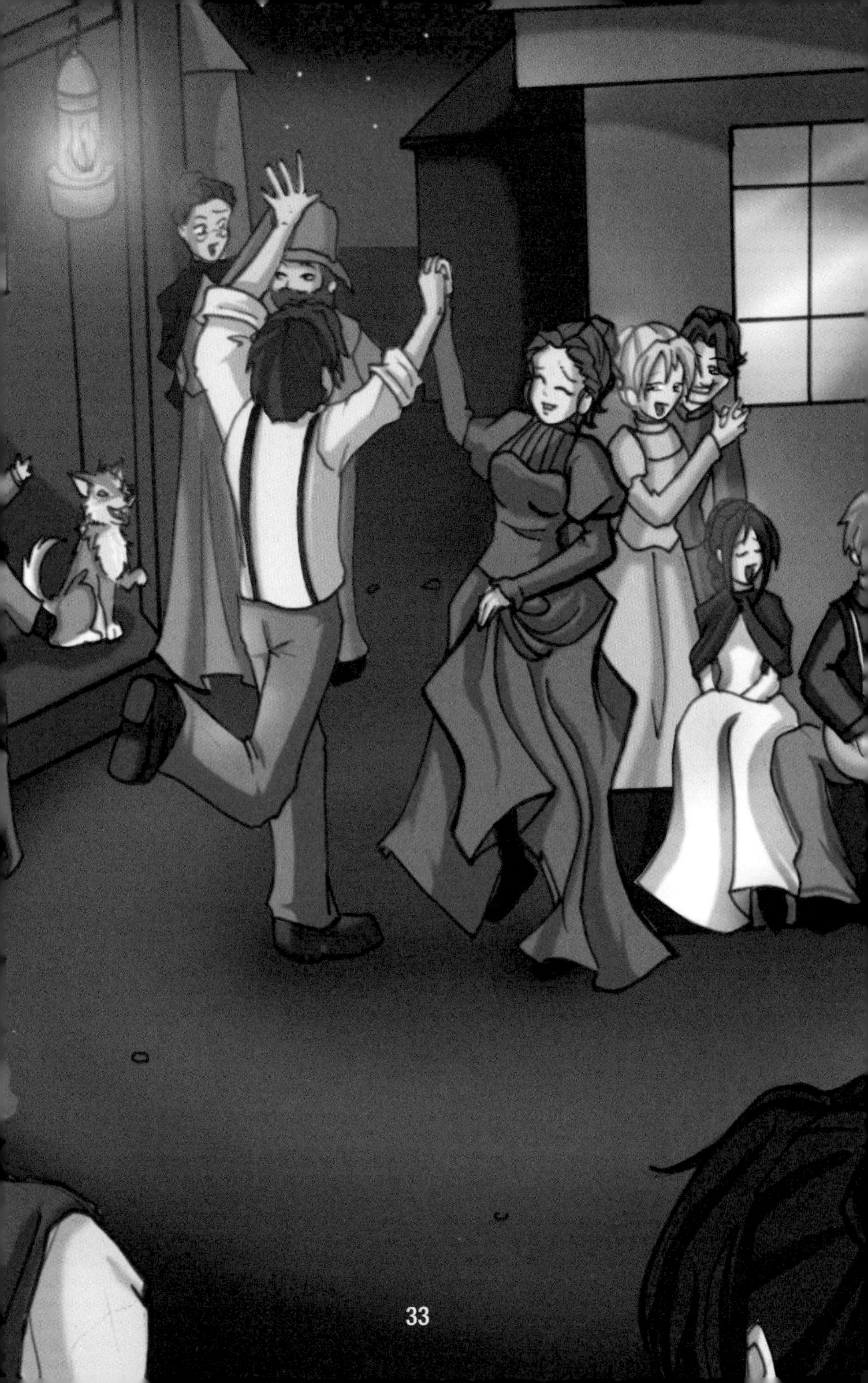

At midnight, Mom and Dad made us go back to the cabin. I suddenly realized how tired I was.

I fell into bed, ready to dream of my gold nuggets and Alaskan huskies.

Late in the night, I woke to the sound of footsteps scraping across the wood floor of our cabin.

I grabbed the nearest and heaviest thing I could find, our family Bible, and raised it over my head.

"Halt!" I cried. "Drop the goods!"

The figure knocked me off my feet.

All the noise woke Cassie up. She saw me on the floor. Then she saw the stranger, and figured out what was happening.

She picked up the heavy Bible and threw it. The stranger was knocked over.

I couldn't believe it. Cassie, my annoying baby sister Cassie, had saved my life.

She bent over the still figure. "Is he dead?"

"I don't know," I said.

Cassie lit the oil lamp on the nightstand to see who it was.

Sugar Gold Charlie rubbed his head.

"That sister of yours has a pretty good arm on her," he said with a grin.

"How could you rob us?" I cried.

You saved my life. You were my hero. My friend.

"You shouldn't steal, you rotten old man," said Cassie.

Charlie looked up at us with a funny expression. "You're right," he said. "I am rotten."

Cassie was angry. She quickly grabbed her coat. "I'm going to tell the police," she said. "They'll lock you up forever!"

Charlie raised his arm. "Wait!" he said. "Please!"

Charlie sat up. He was still holding our gold in his hands.

"Let me tell you something about gold," he said softly. "You can never have enough. You'll always want more."

He handed me the bag. "Sometimes you'll do whatever it takes," he said. "Even if it means you might hurt your friends."

We were all quiet for a moment.

"If we let you go, how do we know you won't steal again?" Cassie demanded.

Charlie lowered his head. The light from the oil lamp gleamed on something wet in his eyes.

"I give you my word," he said. "And all my gold."

"We don't want your gold," Cassie told him. She stared at the Bible. "But we will let you go."

"After all, you did save my brother's life," she added.

"That's right, he did," I said.

Charlie scratched his beard.

Just then, I heard a loud crack. The air around us was warm, and seemed to be growing warmer.

"What's that smell?" Cassie asked.

Chapter 6

Fire and Snow

We heard our dad calling from his room.

"Are you kids, okay?"

Cassie, Charlie, and I all stared at each other. What would Dad say if he came in and found us all together?

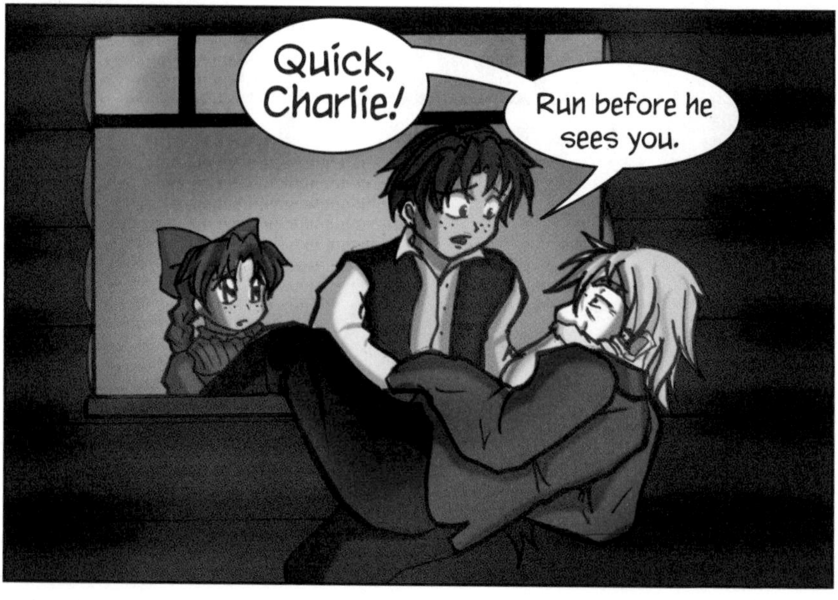
Quick, Charlie!
Run before he sees you.

Charlie escaped just in time.

I watched him disappear into the night just as Dad bounded into our room. "Ethan! Cassie! Grab your things. A fire's coming!" he hollered.

I grabbed our pokes of gold and followed Dad out the door of our cabin.

"Be careful!" yelled Mom.

The fire was immense. Tongues of flames licked the night sky. It looked as if all of Dawson City was in blazes.

I followed Dad down the street as he ran toward the center of town. Along the way, I saw sparks leaping from housetop to housetop. Cinders fell from the dark clouds billowing overhead. There was no way to escape the fire.

People were screaming. Horses were neighing. Dogs ran through the streets.

Lots of people were pushing past us, trying to escape the fire. But in the middle of town, we saw another group of people handing out buckets.

"Grab a bucket!" said my father. "We need to help put out the fire!"

Women and kids were passing buckets from one to another. They were filling them from the river and moving them along the long line to where the fires blazed.

Everyone's faces looked hot and pink in the light of the flames.

Dad and I were going to join the line of the bucket brigade when we heard a man yelling at us. He was standing by a burning building with a hose in his hands.

"Over here! We need help with the hoses!"

"They must be pumping in river water," said Dad. "Come on, let's help."

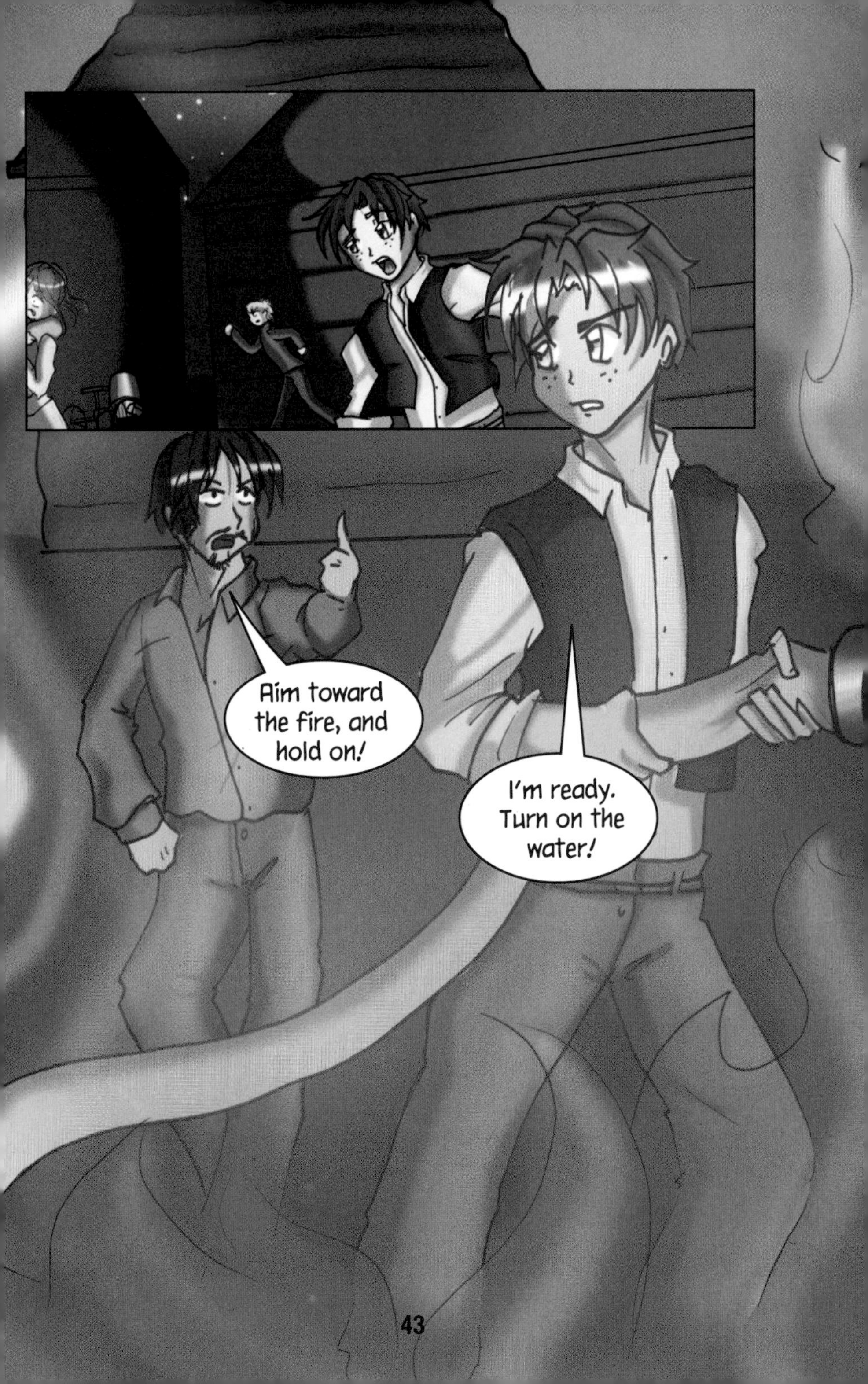
Aim toward the fire, and hold on!
I'm ready. Turn on the water!

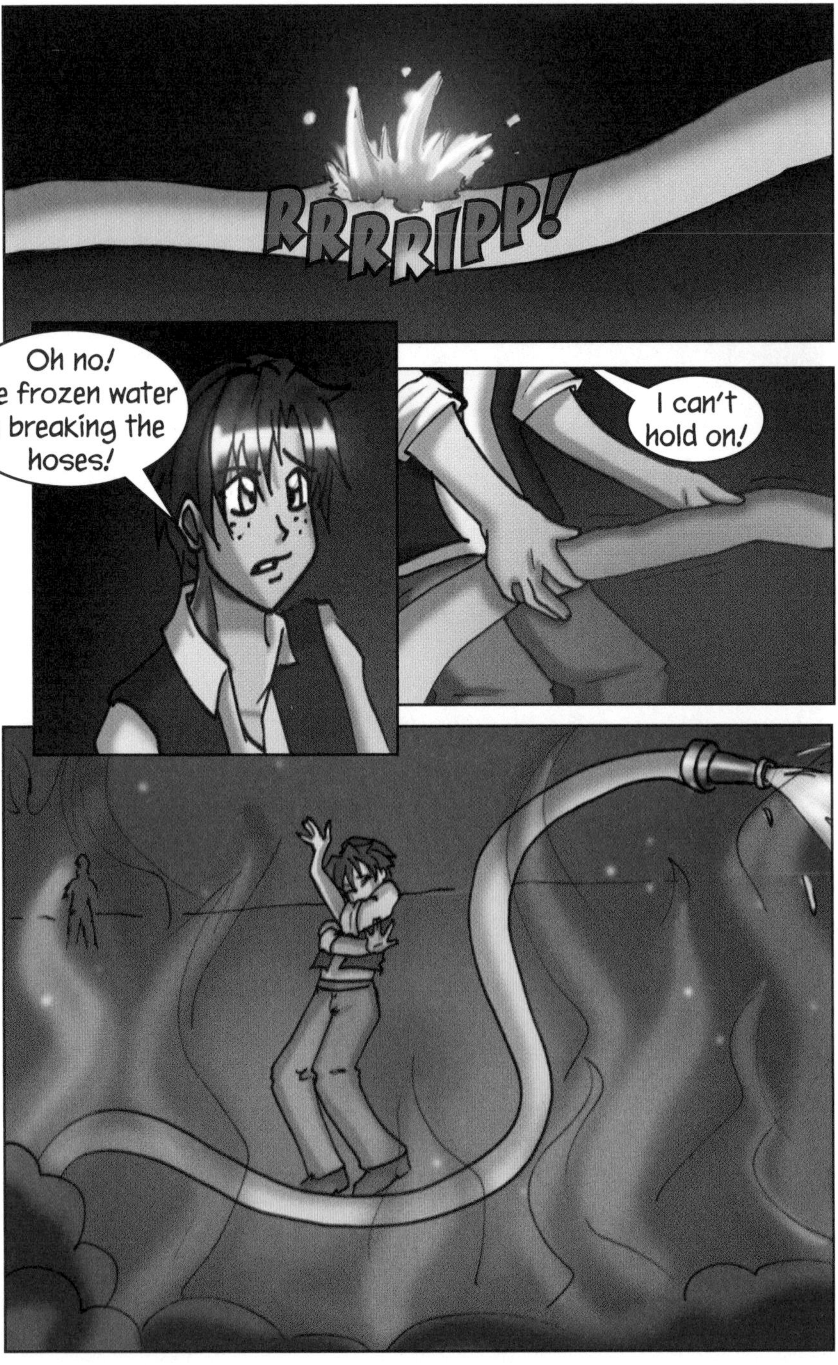
RRRRIPP!
Oh no! The frozen water is breaking the hoses!
I can't hold on!

The hoses seemed to leap from our hands.

Suddenly, I was surrounded by a thick cloud of smoke. I couldn't see anything. A hand grabbed me around my waist.

"Let's get out of here," said Dad.

"But we have to help," I said.

Dad pulled me down the street, out of the smoky clouds.

"Nothing can be done now. Look at it, son. Dawson City is doomed," he said quietly.

He was right. Flames were everywhere. It was getting harder to breathe.

"We need to find Cassie and your mom," said Dad. "I hope they just stayed in the cabin."

Our cabin! Maybe it was far enough from the city to escape the flames. Maybe we would be lucky this time. Maybe we could save our house and survive this disaster.

But we couldn't. By the time we reached our cabin, flames were already devouring it.

We watched helplessly until our home was just a pile of ashes.

"At least we still have our gold," I said, trying to be cheerful.

"Gold is nothing if you don't have a bed," said Cassie.

Dad sighed. "You got your wish, Eliza. We'll go back to our home in Seattle."

Mom took his hand.

"No," she said quietly. "This is our home now."

I looked around at the town. It was just a bunch of burning embers.

"Mom," I said. "Does this mean I can get a dog?"

Dad looked up at the sky that gleamed with flaming gold. "I wonder how Sugar Gold Charlie is doing tonight," he said.

I looked at Cassie and winked.

"Oh, I'm sure he's all right," I said. "He always is."

About the Author

Jessica Gunderson grew up in the small town of Washburn, North Dakota. She has a bachelor's degree from the University of North Dakota and a master's degree in creative writing from Minnesota State University, Mankato. She likes rainy days and thunderstorms. She also likes exploring haunted houses and playing MadLibs. She teaches English in Madison, Wisconsin, where she lives with her cat, Yossarian.

About the Illustrator

When Shannon Townsend discovered anime in 1996, she never dreamed that her hobby would become her career. A self-taught artist, Townsend also works as an instructor, teaching anime and manga style at libraries, museums, and community college events for young people. She has won awards for her work, including First Place in the *Game Pro Magazine* Final Fantasy contest.

GLOSSARY

Alaskan husky (uh-LAS-kun HUS-kee)—a special breed of strong dog used for pulling sleds in Alaska and the far north

billowing (BIL-oh-wing)—rising in large clouds

cinders (SIN-durz)—tiny pieces of burning material

depression (duh-PRESH-un)—a time when many people are out of work and there isn't much money

hardships (HARD-ships)—problems or difficulties

scheme (SKEEM)—a plan

sluice (SLOOS)—a wooden ramp built for running water from a river or stream through it. Gold hunters used sluices to find gold dust and nuggets.

waterfront (WAW-tur-frunt)—the docks of a city; where ships pulled in to unload their cargo and passengers

THE ALASKAN GOLD RUSH

Gold was first discovered in the Klondike and Yukon region near Dawson in 1896. Three men named George Carmack, Skookum Jim, and Dawson Charlie were hiking along Rabbit Creek, when one of them saw a gold nugget along the bank. They stopped and washed some pans of gravel. At the bottom of the pans was more gold than they'd ever seen! Word spread, and the gold rush was on.

The *Portland*, the steamship Ethan and his father saw pull in to Seattle's harbor in July, 1897, carried over one million dollars in gold.

During the gold rush, over 100,000 people flocked to the Klondike region in search of fortune. In the spring of 1897, 1,500 people lived in Dawson City. Within one year, Dawson City's population grew to 30,000.

Gold prospectors weren't the first to settle in the Klondike region. The native people of the region were the Carcross-Tagish Tlingit Indians. They were a blend of the coastal Tlingit Indians and the interior Tagish and Athapaskan Indians.

Order was maintained in Dawson by the North West Mounted Police (now called the Royal Canadian Mounted Police or just "Mounties"). The Mounted Police did more than just enforce the law. They also cared for the sick and collected taxes.

After the fire of 1899, Dawson City was rebuilt. Paved streets and sidewalks were built instead of dirt roads. Many of the new buildings had electricity.

Discussion Questions

1. What are the reasons Ethan's family rushed north in search of gold?

2. What dangers or hardships did Ethan's family face during the gold rush? Can you think of any hardships they may have faced that are not included in the story?

3. Would you have forgiven Sugar Gold Charlie for trying to steal your gold, or would you have told your parents or the police? Describe what choice you would make and why. Do you think Ethan and Cassie made the right decision?

4. What did Cassie mean when she said, "Gold is nothing if you don't have a bed"?

WRITING PROMPTS

1. Avalanche! You've just been trapped in a giant pile of snow. How did it happen? What does it feel like? How do you escape?

2. If you discovered gold what would you do? Would you keep it a secret or tell your friends? Would you buy something right away or save up for something else?

3. Ethan and Cassie were brave the night they faced the intruder in their home. But what if the intruder was someone else instead of Sugar Gold Charlie? How would they have acted? Write down what you think could have happened that night.

ALSO PUBLISHED BY STONE ARCH BOOKS

HOT IRON
The Adventures of a Civil War Powder Boy

Twelve-year-old Charlie O'Leary signs aboard the *USS Varuna* as it steams its way toward the mouth of the Mississippi River to fight the Confederate Navy. Charlie is short enough, and swift enough, to race through the crowded ship and fetch gunpowder for the big guns on deck. The cannons boom like thunder. Their hot iron shells blast through enemy ships, ripping canvas, wood, and metal. Charlie hopes to find his brother Johnny among the *Varuna*'s fleet. But will their ships survive the awesome Battle of New Orleans?

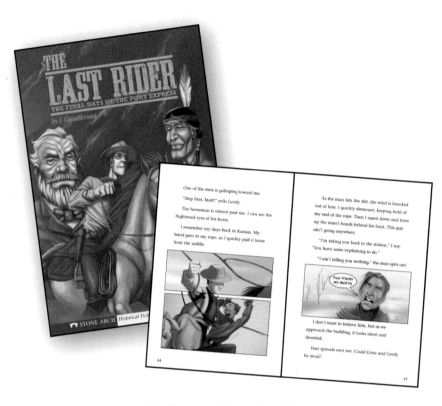

THE LAST RIDER
The Final Days of the Pony Express

Matt Edgars hungers for adventure. The Pony Express is the answer to his dreams. Riding fast, riding far, he brings the mail to settlers scattered across the Nevada and Utah deserts. Matt can handle the punishing sun and the poisonous rattlesnakes, but he's worried about rumors of a war with the Paiute nation. Then someone begins setting the Express stations on fire. Are these the last days for the young riders?

Internet Sites

Do you want to know more about subjects related to this book? Or are you interested in learning about other topics? Then check out FactHound, a fun, easy way to find Internet sites.

Our investigative staff has already sniffed out great sites for you!

Here's how to use FactHound:

1. Visit *www.facthound.com*

2. Select your grade level.

3. To learn more about subjects related to this book, type in the book's ISBN number: **1598893106**.

4. Click the **Fetch It** button.

FactHound will fetch the best Internet sites for you.